Dear Parents and Educators,

Welcome to Penguin Young Readers! As parents and educators, you know that each child develops at his or her own pace—in terms of speech, critical thinking, and, of course, reading. Penguin Young Readers recognizes this fact. As a result, each Penguin Young Readers book is assigned a traditional easy-to-read level (1–4) as well as a Guided Reading Level (A–P). Both of these systems will help you choose the right book for your child. Please refer to the back of each book for specific leveling information. Penguin Young Readers features esteemed authors and illustrators, stories about favorite characters, fascinating nonfiction, and more!

Fox in Love

LEVEL **3**

GUIDED READING LEVEL **J**

This book is perfect for a **Transitional Reader** who:
• can read multisyllable and compound words;
• can read words with prefixes and suffixes;
• is able to identify story elements (beginning, middle, end, plot, setting, characters, problem, solution); and
• can understand different points of view.

Here are some **activities** you can do during and after reading this book:
• Making Inferences: Making an inference involves using what you know to make a guess about what you don't know, or reading between the lines. Make inferences to answer the following questions:
    • On pages 15 and 16, why does Louise give Fox looks?
    • On page 33, why does Raisin run off?
    • On page 38, why is Raisin mad?
• Creative Writing: In the last story in this book, Raisin can't compete in the dance contest with Fox because she gets sick. Pretend you are Fox and write a get well card to Raisin. While you are writing, think about Fox's relationship with Raisin. What would he say to her to make her feel better?

Remember, sharing the love of rec   ft you can give!

—Bonnie Bader, EdM
   Penguin Young Readers program

*Penguin Young Readers are leveled by independent reviewers applying the standards developed by Irene Fountas and Gay Su Pinnell in *Matching Books to Readers: Using Leveled Books in Guided Reading*, Heinemann, 1999.

For Benedict Clouette

Penguin Young Readers
Published by the Penguin Group
Penguin Group (USA) Inc., 375 Hudson Street, New York, New York 10014, USA
Penguin Group (Canada), 90 Eglinton Avenue East, Suite 700, Toronto, Ontario M4P 2Y3, Canada
(a division of Pearson Penguin Canada Inc.)
Penguin Books Ltd., 80 Strand, London WC2R 0RL, England
Penguin Group Ireland, 25 St. Stephen's Green, Dublin 2, Ireland (a division of Penguin Books Ltd.)
Penguin Group (Australia), 250 Camberwell Road, Camberwell, Victoria 3124, Australia
(a division of Pearson Australia Group Pty. Ltd.)
Penguin Books India Pvt. Ltd., 11 Community Centre, Panchsheel Park, New Delhi—110 017, India
Penguin Group (NZ), 67 Apollo Drive, Rosedale, Auckland 0632, New Zealand
(a division of Pearson New Zealand Ltd.)
Penguin Books (South Africa) (Pty.) Ltd., 24 Sturdee Avenue,
Rosebank, Johannesburg 2196, South Africa

Penguin Books Ltd., Registered Offices: 80 Strand, London WC2R 0RL, England

Text copyright © 1982 by Edward Marshall. Pictures copyright © 1982 by James Marshall. All rights
reserved. First published in 1982 by Dial Books for Young Readers, an imprint of Penguin Group (USA) Inc.
Published in a Puffin Easy-to-Read edition in 1994. Published in 2012 by Penguin Young Readers,
an imprint of Penguin Group (USA) Inc., 345 Hudson Street, New York, New York 10014.
Manufactured in China.

The Library of Congress has catalogued the Dial edition
under the following Control Number: 82070190

ISBN 978-0-14-036843-7   10 9

FOX IN LOVE

by Edward Marshall
pictures by James Marshall

Penguin Young Readers
An Imprint of Penguin Group (USA) Inc.

Contents

FOX IN LUCK

"Fox, dear," said Fox's mom.

"What did I do?" said Fox.

"I want you to take Louise
to the park," said Mom.

"I'm too busy," said Fox.

"You'll take Louise," said Mom.

"And that is that."

"No!" said Fox.

Mom gave Fox one of her looks.

"Oh, all right," said Fox.

"Of all the luck.

Come on, Louise."

"Tra-la-la-la," said Louise.

At the park

Louise had quite a bit of fun.

She played in the sandbox.

She hung upside down.

She played on the slide.

And she played on the swings.

"This is dumb," said Fox.

"Let's go home and watch TV."

Just then they saw

a pretty white fox.

She was all alone.

And she was having a fine time.

"Wow!" said Fox.

"She looks just like a movie star!"

"Hi!" said the pretty white fox.

"My name is Raisin."

All of a sudden Fox could not speak.

He forgot his own name.

"Hi!" said Louise.

"I'm Louise.

And this is my brother Fox."

Fox and Louise got on

the merry-go-round.

"You are sweet to bring

your little sister to the park,"

said Raisin.

"I love to do it," said Fox.

Louise gave Fox a look.

"This is more fun than TV,"
said Raisin.

"Oh, yes," said Fox.

"I never watch TV."

Louise gave Fox another look.

"Oh, dear," said Raisin.

"I am late for my piano lesson."

"I love the piano," said Fox.

"See you again," said Raisin.

And she left the park.

"Wow!" said Fox.

The next day

Fox found Louise in her room.

"Time for the park," he said.

"I'm too busy," said Louise.

"You can bring your dolly," said Fox.

"She doesn't like the park,"
said Louise.

"You are going to the park," said Fox.
"And that is *that!*"

"You can't make me!" said Louise.

"I will buy you a hot dog," said Fox.

"With onions."

"Let's go," said Louise.

And off they went.

At the park, Fox spent his last dime.

"There's Raisin," said Louise.

"Hello," said Raisin.

"I love hot dogs!"

"Oh, dear," said Fox.

"I just spent my last dime."

And he gave Louise such a look!

"Then I will buy you a hot dog,"
said Raisin.

"I am very rich."

"Wow!" said Fox.

"This is my lucky day!"

FOX AND THE GIRLS

On Monday

Fox and Millie went to the fair.

"Let's have our picture taken,"
said Fox.

"Oh, yes, let's do," said Millie.

Click went the camera.

And out came the pictures.

"Sweet," said Millie.

"One for you and one for me,"
said Fox.

On Tuesday

Fox and Rose went to the fair.

"How about some pictures?"

said Fox.

"Tee-hee," said Rose.

Click went the camera.

And out came the pictures.

"Tee-hee," said Rose.

"I'll keep mine always,"
said Fox.

On Wednesday

Fox and Lola went to the fair.

"I don't have a picture of us,"

said Fox.

"Follow me," said Lola.

Click went the camera.

And out came the pictures.

"What fun!" said Lola.

"I'll carry mine everywhere."

"Me too," said Fox.

On Thursday

Fox and Raisin went to the fair.

"Ooh! I want a picture," said Raisin.

"Fine idea," said Fox.

Click went the camera.

And out came the pictures.

"Don't we look silly,"

said Raisin.

"A scream," said Fox.

The next day Fox was
showing off for Raisin.

And some pictures
fell out of his pocket.
Raisin picked them up.

"Well!" she cried.
"Wait until the girls
hear about this!"
And on Saturday
Fox went to the fair . . .

All alone.

Click.

FOX
TROT

Fox was a fine dancer.

He could waltz.

He could boogie.

He could do the stomp.

"That Fox really moves!" said Dexter.

One day Fox decided to enter

THE BIG DANCE CONTEST.

"Who will be my partner?" he asked.

"Don't look at me," said Carmen.

"I don't dance."

"Why not ask Raisin?" said Dexter.

"She's a great dancer."

"She's mad about something,"
said Fox.

"Ask her anyway," said Carmen.

"Here she comes now."

"Uh," said Fox.

"Yes, what is it?" said Raisin.

"Will you be my partner in

THE BIG DANCE CONTEST?"

asked Fox.

"Are you sure you are good enough?"

said Raisin.

"Don't worry about *that*!" said Fox.

Every day Fox and Raisin

practiced hard for

THE BIG DANCE CONTEST.

They did the waltz.

They did the boogie.

They did the stomp.

They even did the Fox trot.

Raisin was very good.

But she was still mad

about something.

"I'm sure they will win

first prize," said Dexter.

41

On the day of

THE BIG DANCE CONTEST,

Fox went to Raisin's house.

"Sorry, Fox," said Raisin's mom.

"Raisin has the mumps."

"Oh no!" cried Fox.

Fox went home.

He sat down

in front of the TV.

But he didn't even turn it on.

He was too upset.

Suddenly he had an idea.

"Come here, Louise!" he cried.

"What did I do?" said Louise.

"Just do what I say," said Fox.

"First put your right foot here.

And then put your left foot there."

Louise did as she was told.

Louise was a fast learner.

Soon they were dancing

around the room.

Fox looked at his watch.

"Let's go!" he cried.

THE BIG DANCE CONTEST was on.

"Fox and his partner are next,"
called out the judge.

Fox was nervous.

"Calm down," said Louise.

And the music began.

Fox and Louise did the waltz.

They did the boogie.

They did the stomp.

And the crowd went wild.

"How did you do?" said Dexter.

"We won second prize," said Fox.

"Next year we will win first!"
said Louise.

"You said it!" said Fox.